First published in Belgium and Holland by Clavis Uitgeverij, Hasselt — Amsterdam, 2016
Copyright © 2016, Clavis Uitgeverij

English translation from the Dutch by Clavis Publishing Inc. New York
Copyright © 2016 for the English language edition: Clavis Publishing Inc. New York

Visit us on the web at www.clavisbooks.com

Larry & Lola. What Will We See There? written by Elly van der Linden and illustrated by Suzanne Diederen
Original title: *Lasse & Lina. Wat zien we daar?*
Translated from the Dutch by Clavis Publishing

ISBN 978-1-60537-286-0

This book was printed in April 2016 at Wai Man Book Binding (China) Ltd. Flat A, 9/F., Phase 1,
Kwun Tong Industrial Centre, 472-484 Kwun Tong Road, Kwun Tong, Kowloon, H.K.

First Edition
10 9 8 7 6 5 4 3 2 1

Larry & Lola

What Will We See There?

Clavis

NEW YORK

Elly van der Linden
& Suzanne Diederen

We are **Larry and Lola!**
It's a busy day today.
We are going to the zoo.

Which animals do you like?
What doesn't belong in the zoo?
What will we see there?

And what is Mikey the mouse doing?

Look! An elephant, a zebra and lions.
Cheerful monkeys wave and shriek.

Which animals do we see here?
And which things don't you see?

We are **Larry and Lola!**
Want to go for a walk?
We are going to the woods.

What do you see when you're in the woods?
What will you definitely not see?
What will we see there?

What do we see here in the woods?
And which things aren't here?

And what is Mikey the mouse doing?

Walking over winding paths,
picking up acorns and leaves.

We are **Larry and Lola!**
We are going to feed the animals
in the petting zoo.

What doesn't belong in the petting zoo?
Which animals do you recognize?
What will we see there?

And what is Mikey the mouse doing?

Tickling the rabbits and petting the sheep,
waving at the little horse. What fun!

Which animals do we see here in the petting zoo?
And which things don't you see here?

We are **Larry and Lola!**
Hooray!
We are going to
the playground.

What do you like to do at the playground?
What don't you need at the playground?
What will we see there?

What are we playing with?
What don't you see here?

And what is Mikey the mouse doing?

Going down the slide and sitting on the seesaw,
riding on the wobbly chicken.

We are **Larry and Lola!**
The weather is nice today.
We are going to the beach.

What do you need at the beach?
And what don't you need to take with you?
What will we see there?

What do you see here at the seaside?
What don't you see here?

And what is Mikey the mouse doing?

Sunny beach, wind and waves,
digging holes in the sand.

We are **Larry and Lola!**
We like to do tricks.
Now we're going
to the circus too.

What do you like about the circus?
And what doesn't belong there?
What will we see there?

What is happening here at the circus?
And what don't you need here?

And what is Mikey the mouse doing?

Clever animals doing tricks,
throwing balls and swinging through the air.